CARTOON NETWORK

SCOOBY-DOO'S™

GUIDE TO SCHOOL

BY HOWIE DEWIN

SCHOLASTIC INC.

New York Toronto London Auckland Sydney
Mexico City New Delhi Hong Kong Buenos Aires

ISBN 0-439-43817-9

Design by Bethany Dixon

12 11 10 9 8 7 6 5 4 3 2 1 2 3 4 5 6 7/0

Printed in the U.S.A.
First Scholastic printing, September 2002

"What's Your Look?"

THE MYSTERY GIRL

Chapter One
By Daphne

I love the first day of school. There are so many great new things — clothes, classes, clothes, clubs . . . and did I mention clothes?

Actually, the thing I like best is meeting new people. Every year there are sure to be new students and new teachers. I like to get to know them and show them around.

That's why it was so great when Fred and I were called into the principal's office right after homeroom on the first day of school this year.

"Fred, Daphne," the principal said. "I want to ask you to be the official welcoming committee for all the new students this year."

"Cool," said Fred. "Happy to do it, sir."

"Absolutely," I agreed. "Can we throw a party?"

"I leave it up to you," answered the principal. "Here's a list of all the new students. I trust you will make contact with each of them this week?"

"You bet," I told him, and we all shook hands.

I looked at the list as Fred and I headed to class.

"It looks like there are only five new students so far, Fred," I said. "We should be able to meet all of them today, don't you think?"

"We can get together at lunch to figure out how we should divide the list between us," Fred suggested.

"Okay," I agreed, "but if I see anyone new before then, I might just introduce myself."

"Good thinking. See you later," Fred said. He headed to his class and I headed to mine.

That was the first time I saw one of the new girls. She wore a long green corduroy coat and she had a scarf over her head. She walked with a bit of slump and she had her head down.

Wow, I thought, *she really needs me!*

Not only is she new, but she's obviously lonely. And she could really do with a fashion makeover.

"Miss?" I called out to her.

She seemed to jump a little, and then she started moving in the opposite direction.

"Miss! I just want to say hi!" I said.

I followed after her as fast as my shiny new pumps would allow, but I'm afraid that wasn't fast enough.

The mystery girl put her head down even lower and ran around the corner toward the gym.

By the time I got to the corner myself, she was gone.

TO BE CONTINUED

Fashion Doo's (and Don'ts)

Whether you're in class or off solving a crime, it's always helpful to look good. A few simple rules will go a long way to making you a fashion trendsetter!

DOO be sure your clothes fit.

DOO be sure your clothes match.

DOO be sure your clothes are clean.

DOO be sure your clothes are on.

Once you've got your clothes under control, it's time to think about the way you like things to appear. Look around you. In school, there are only a couple of places where you can really express who you are through decoration — your locker, your desk, your books. (Be sure to ask your teacher if it's okay before you do anything to any school property.)

MAKE YOUR OWN BOOK COVERS

Making a nice cover for your schoolbooks not only gives you a way to express yourself artistically, but also helps protect your books.

You can use stretchy fabric and thread or paper and tape. Try a solid color fabric and decorate it with fabric-safe markers, or use a patterned fabric and let the pattern be your decoration. If you use paper, you can do anything from coloring to collage to stenciling. Think about what you like to look at because you're going to be staring at your books all year long! Whatever you decide, the first few steps are the same:

Measure the book you want to cover two different ways:

- First, measure it from top to bottom with a ruler. Add one inch. Write down the number.
- Second, with a tape measure, measure from the outside edge of the front cover, around the spine, to the outside edge of the back cover. Add two inches. Write down that number.

Cut a piece of stretchy material or paper to that exact size.

Decorate your cover in whatever way you want. Maybe you want to cut out your initials and sew or paste them on the front cover. Perhaps you want to make a collage of magazine clippings. Whatever you want to say about yourself — here's the place to say it.

Seal the seams of your cover:

Lay the paper or fabric facedown lengthwise on a flat surface. Along the side edges, measure in one inch. Fold the cover along those lines. Along the top and bottom edges, measure in a half inch. Fold the cover along those lines.

For fabric: Pin the fabric in place after folding it. Using a needle and thread, stitch along the top and bottom edges to hold the folded fabric in place. (You may want to ask a parent for help.)

For paper: Tape down the top and bottom edges to hold the folded paper in place.

Slip the front folded cover edge over the front cover of your book. Wrap it around to the back. Pull open the back cover and slip the back folded cover edge over the back cover.

That's it! You're finished.

Lock in Your Look With a Locker Worth Looking At!

The inside of your locker says a lot about you. Is it neat and organized, or do moldy sandwiches fall out when you open the door? Do you have a picture of you and your gang taped to the inside of the door? Is there a football where your books should be? Is there a mirror hanging from the top of the door so you can check your hair?

The first thing you should do before jazzing up your locker is be sure your school allows it. If it does, then here are some ideas:

Sports Nut?

Hang a mini-baseball or football from a hook. Keep a chart of stats from your favorite team that you can update. Find a couple of action photos to cover the inside of the door. Put up an inspirational quote or two from your favorite coach or athlete.

Movie Buff?

Put up pictures of your favorite movie stars. Write down one or two of your favorite lines from the movies and tape them up. Attach a pad of paper to the door so you can keep a list of the movies you've seen and the ones you want to see.

Model Student?

Post your class schedule. Hang a pad of paper to jot down homework assignments. Tape up an envelope to collect all your papers with great grades and comments on them. Keep a small box of different kinds of pens, pencils, and other supplies.

Or mix up these ideas and come up with others! It's up to you.

Think about the people, places, and things that inspire you. If you decorate your locker with these ideas in mind, then you'll always head off to class ready to achieve!

Perk Up Your Backpack!

You carry it around every day — your backpack should say a little bit about you.

Personally, I have a collection of ribbons that I change every day so my backpack always matches my outfit. But you can do whatever works for you.

If it's okay with your parents, get some fabric markers and do a little doodling.

If you're handy with a needle and thread, you could sew on some patches.

And you don't have to do much of anything if you just clip on a few key-chain characters.

There are stickers and beads and ribbons and a million other things to put on your backpack that will make lugging those big books around a lot more fun!

Cool Rules for Getting to School in Style

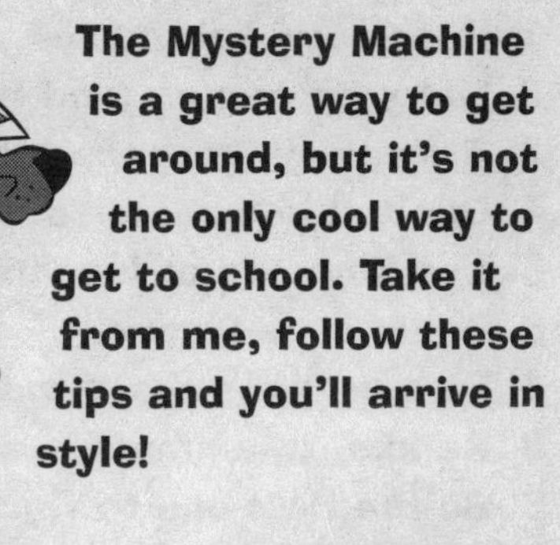

The Mystery Machine is a great way to get around, but it's not the only cool way to get to school. Take it from me, follow these tips and you'll arrive in style!

If you make the hike by **BIKE** — wear a helmet.

You won't be late if you **SKATE** — and wear a helmet **AND** knee, elbow, and wrist pads.

It's a hoot to do it by **SCOOT**-er — but make sure to walk it when you cross the street.

You won't have to rush if you take the **BUS** — just remember to stay in your seat.

It won't seem far if you ride by **CAR** — as long as you wear your seat belt.

And if you **WALK**, you'll have time to talk — just don't do it with strangers.

Remember — it's cool to be careful!

Top Ten Ways to Look GREAT!

1. Keep your hair out of your eyes.
2. Get your beauty (and brain) sleep.
3. Stay away from the lunchroom candy machines.
4. Don't skip gym class.
5. Use a napkin at lunchtime.
6. Smile at everyone.
7. Be sure your shoes match.
8. Be kind to animals — especially nervous dogs.
9. Be the first one to figure out a clue — or any answer.
10. Try very hard not to fall down trapdoors and get chased by ghouls.

Fred's File

"Do What You Do Best!"

The Mystery Girl

Chapter Two
By Fred

As a natural-born leader, I'm always happy to take on assignments like the one the principal gave Daphne and me this year. It's nice to welcome new people. It also gives me a chance to secure their votes for class president.

It didn't take much time. I met three of the five new students before I even got to class. They were all lost and searching for their new classes.

The first one I met was Phil, a nice guy from out of state. He introduced me to Peggy, who had just moved from the other side of town. They'd gotten lost together. Peggy shook my hand with a firm grip and asked if I knew anything about the debate team. I told her I would find out for her, but that right now I had to get to class.

I gave them exact directions to their classes and sent them on their way.

Then I ran into a girl named Susan Oleson. She was from Texas and had this great southern accent. She had really long blonde hair and bright blue eyes. I decided I should probably walk her all the way to her class. I was just being a gentleman.

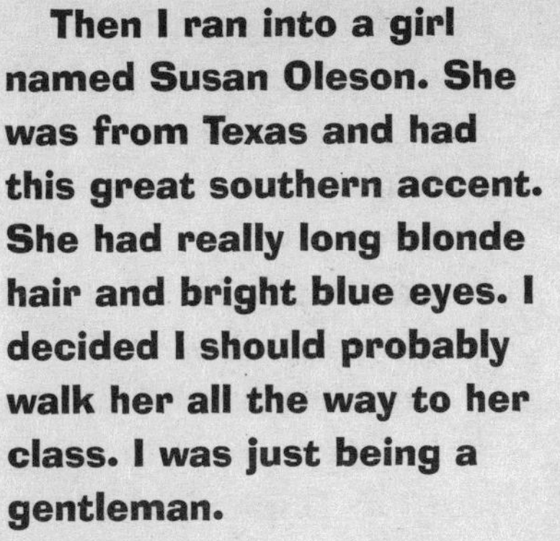

Anyway, after Susan was settled, I finally set off to my class.

That's when I saw her, another new girl. She was wearing a long green corduroy coat and a scarf over her head. She walked with a bit of slump and she had her head down.

"Can I help you?" I called out, but the girl didn't even turn around. In fact, she seemed to hurry away from me. I was really late for class by now, so I decided to wait until lunch to meet her.

Daphne and I met up with the gang a couple of hours later in the cafeteria.

"I met a really great new guy in my math class," Daphne said before we'd even sat down.

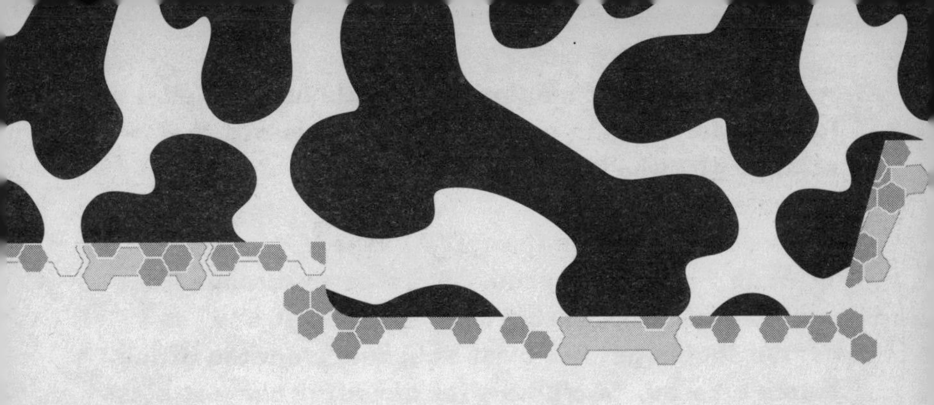

"What's up?" Velma asked.

We told her about our assignment from the principal.

"Cool," said Shaggy, who was already wolfing down his second sandwich.

"So let's go over the list," Daphne said. "Phil Howard."

"I met him already," I said, "along with Peggy Ward."

"Susan Oleson," Daphne said.

"I met her, too," I said.

"I guess you did," said Velma. She must have noticed that I was smiling a little.

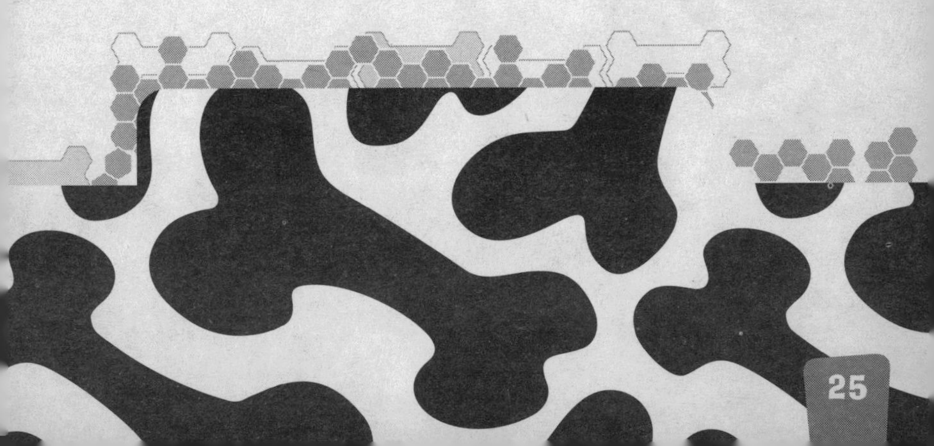

"Fine," said Daphne, looking a little hurt. "Well, I met Rob Snyder in math class, so that just leaves the strange girl who ran away. That must be Cindy Reynolds."

"Corduroy coat and scarf?" I asked.

"Yeah," agreed Daphne. "She was so strange."

"I saw her, too," I told her. "Must be shy."

"We should get her class schedule from the office," Velma offered. "We'll wait for her after her last class and talk to her then."

Just then, a tall, dark-haired girl in a bright red dress approached our table.

"Excuse me," she said, "but Susan Oleson told me that you were in charge of meeting all the new students."

"That's right," I said. "We're the welcoming committee."

"Well, I thought I'd save you the trouble of tracking me down. I'm Cindy Reynolds. I just moved here from Michigan."

We all looked at her, a little confused. This was definitely not the girl I had seen.

"Wow. Well, welcome," Daphne said. "It's nice to meet you. Thanks for introducing yourself."

"Sure thing," she smiled.

"We're going to organize a party for later in the week. We'll let you know as soon as it's set."

"Great," she said. "Bye!" She walked away. She wasn't slouching at all.

"Hmmm," Velma said, "looks like we've got a mystery."

"I'll say," I said.

The bell rang before we could discuss it any further. We all headed toward our next classes and agreed that we'd work on our new mystery after school.

We were just about to split up when Velma saw someone at the end of the hall.

"Is that her?" she asked.

There she was. Walking quickly past the science lab.

"Hey!" I shouted. "Miss!"

She took off like a shot. That girl could really run!

"Let's split up," I suggested.

We all ran off in opposite directions. This time, she wouldn't get away!

TO BE CONTINUED

Top Ten Ways to Be Gym-class Cool

1. **Always play hard!**
2. **Always wear your gym clothes.**
3. **Always be sure your gym clothes are clean!**
4. **Always congratulate the winner.**
5. **Don't cheat or play dirty.**
6. **Make sure your hair looks good.**
7. **Baggy is cool, but make sure your pants stay up!**
8. **Don't sit on the bench.**
9. **Always be willing to learn something new.**
10. **If it's up to you to pick a team, choose the person who never gets picked.**

An Organized Guide to Getting Organized

As a teen detective, I've got to be organized. The tiniest clue can solve the biggest mystery. So, here are some things I do to keep things in order at school.

HOMEWORK NOTEBOOK

Carry this with you to all your classes. When the teacher gives an assignment, write it down as carefully as you'd write down an important clue.

CALENDAR

I tape a monthly calendar to my notebook so I can mark down test dates and other important upcoming events. If you're busy with after-school activities, it's a great place to write down those things, too. That way, you'll know if you haven't left enough time for homework!

FILE FOLDER

I use this for all those papers that get passed around by teachers — study sheets, permission slips, quizzes, and tests (after they're graded . . . yikes!). If I put them in my folder, I don't lose them and I can go through them at the end of the day.

THE LOCKER/BACKPACK CONNECTION

It's no mystery that it's easier to find things in an organized locker than it is in a messy one. The same goes for your backpack. In my locker, I keep books and notebooks stacked by subject. Then, when I get a homework assignment that requires a specific book, I put it in my backpack right away so I don't forget it at the end of the day.

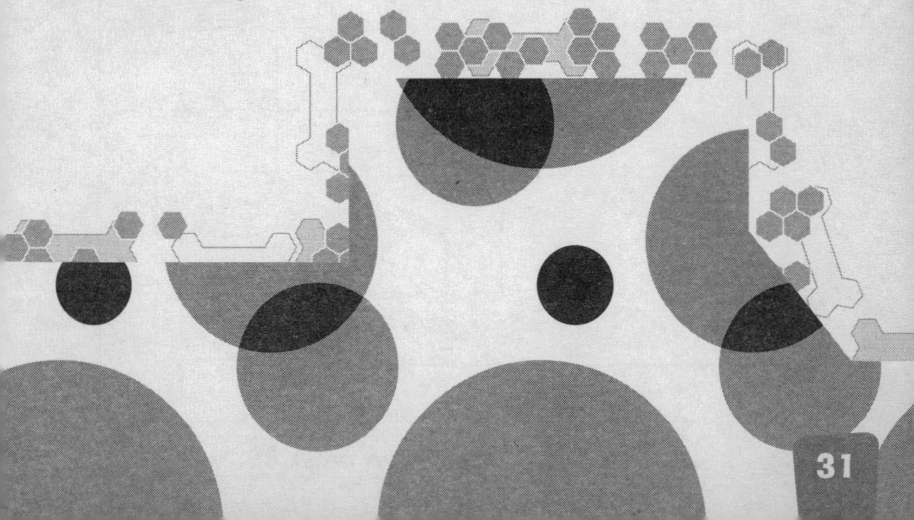

Where the Girls Are!

Can you get Fred from the front door of school to his class on time and make sure he says hello to all the girls on the way? Be sure to time yourself!

(Maze answer on page 80.)

1–3 minutes: Congratulations! Fred got to class early and even had time to recheck his homework.

4–6 minutes: Whew! Fred's on time, but just barely. Good thing he got all his homework done last night!

7–9 minutes: Uh-oh! Fred's late. But at least he made it.

More than 9 minutes: Fred's so late, he might as well go right to lunch. Can you get him back to the cafeteria?

Are You the Leader of the Pack?

As the leader of my gang, I can tell you it's a big responsibility. Are you a leader? Take this quiz and find out.

1. Your friend has something new to show you, but to see it you have to follow him/her to an unfamiliar neighborhood. Do you:

A) trust your friend and do exactly what he or she says?

B) trust your friend, but ask where you're going before you agree to go?

C) tell your friend that you need to know where you're going to go before you decide whether you'll go?

D) tell your friend you don't do anything that other people tell you to do?

2. What do you think about student government?

A) It's a good thing. I campaign for other people.

B) I'm all for it. I've run for office but haven't won yet.

C) It's great. I've held office and really enjoyed it.

D) I think it's stupid and I wish it didn't exist.

3. You've been chosen to pick your own team for a basketball game in gym class. Do you:

A) pick all your friends?
B) pick the very best players you can get?
C) pick people with different strengths and weaknesses?
D) pick the most popular kids?

4. Your teacher has been called out of the classroom. It's quiet for a minute, but then people start to talk and get up from their seats. Before long, things are getting a little wild. Do you:

A) talk quietly with your friend nearby?
B) jump to the front of the class and give spitball lessons?
C) sit with your head on your desk?
D) suggest in a strong voice that everyone should sit down and listen to you because you're going to continue where the teacher left off?

**5. You and your friends are on a hike in the woods. You take a wrong turn and now you're lost.
Do you:**

A) wait for someone to come up with an idea and then support that person?
B) sit down on a rock and worry about your friends?
C) remember all the survival tactics you've ever learned and use the setting sun to figure out which way you should walk to get you and your friends out of the woods?
D) decide which way you think is right, warn your friends they better listen to you, and then take off on your own?

Answer Key to Leader Quiz

If you answered A to three or more questions, you're probably more comfortable letting someone else take the lead, but you're smart enough to make sure that person is worthy of leading.

If you answered B to three or more questions, you know how to be the leader and you do it when it's necessary. But sometimes it's easier to let others do it. You're willing to listen to other people when they have good ideas.

If you answered C to three or more questions, you're a natural leader. You probably always take the lead in any situation you're in.

If you answered D to three or more questions, you have the ability to lead, but you have to be careful not to boss people around. Sometimes the best way to lead is by example.

Scooby's News

The Mystery Girl

Chapter Three
By Scooby

**Ri ras rowhere rear rhe rhool rerause rogs rare rot rallowed ro ro ro rhool.
Ri rave ro ridea rho rhat rirl ras.**

Scooby R-Interpretation:

**I was nowhere near the school because dogs are not allowed to go to school.
I have no idea who that girl was.**

Who Are You This Year?

Scooby-Due

Scooby-Dew

Scooby-Deux

Scooby-Dude

Scooby-Doo

Scooby says, "Just be yourself!"

Rah-ha-ha! Scooby's Favorite School Jokes

The science teacher asked, "What sits on the floor of the ocean and shakes?" Shaggy raised his hand and said, "Like, a nervous wreck?"

What does Scooby look for in a book?
Something he can really sink his teeth into.

Why shouldn't you whisper in class?
Because it's not aloud!

Just for kicks, Velma stood in front of her class at show-and-tell and said, "Every sentence I speak is a lie." Why is that impossible?

Because if every sentence she speaks is a lie, then so is that one — if she's lying about always lying, then she doesn't lie. Jinkies!

BOYS SOCK CAN

Can you scramble these letters around to make a different two-word phrase? I bet Scooby could! The correct answer is at the bottom of the page.

R-ongue R-wisters! Say 'em five times fast!

SCOOBY SCARFS SCOOBY SNACKS
SHAGGY THREW THREE FREE THROWS
SUCH SLOPPY SPEECH AS SCOOBY SPEAKS
FRED'S FRESH FISH FREEZER

Q: Why did Scooby cross the road?
A: He didn't. The Scooby Snack was already on his side of the road!

Scooby Snack

Want to Be in the Drama Club? That Is the Question.

Ravo! Ravo! Rencore!

Those are my ravorite words! Ri rave played rots and rots of different roles in my work as a rime-busting chowhound. Ri'm rot nearly as rervous rhen Ri retend to be romeone else. It's r-r-r-really fun. These are some of my ravorite parts . . .

Pirate Pup

Royal Ruff-Ruff

Ron't be rervous. Rollow my radvice and take a bow-wow:

AUDITION ADVICE:

Convince a friend or two to audition with you. (Everything is more fun with a friend.)

Imagine that all the people who are watching you are sitting in their underwear. (People in their underwear are hard to take too seriously!)

Try out for a part that seems very different from you. (It's not as nerve-wracking if you feel like someone else.)

REHEARSAL ADVICE:

Memorize your lines as soon as you can. (It's easier to believe you're someone else if you aren't holding a book and reading lines.)

Pick out a pair of shoes that seem right for your character and only wear them when you're rehearsing. (It will help you "feel" like that person.)

Really listen to the other people onstage when they're speaking. (It will help you forget you're onstage.)

PERFORMANCE ADVICE:

Take a deep breath and try to relax. When you step onstage you might feel nervous for a minute, but it will probably go away very quickly. Have a great time!

Dear Scooby...
Advice for intelligent dogs

Dear Scooby,

How can I get an education when I'm not allowed in school?

Sincerely, Barking for Books

Rear Barking,

Rou rould ry what Ri've rone. Show off rour racting ability and the Rama Rub might let you ray the rog in the rhool ray. Or risplay a rift for Frisbee-ratching and someone might just bring you in for row-and-tell. The rey is to ret your paw in the door. Ronce you're in, reep your ears rup and risten! You're bow-wound to rearn something.

Dear Scooby,

I am already man's best friend. How can I be a good study companion, too?

Signed, Homework Hound

Rear Homework,

Rirst of all, ron't reat the homework — runless someone rasks you to. Ry not to rool on the rooks rand ron't bury your student's rackpack. Rother rhan that, rust do what you do best — rurl up and go to sleep ro your student ran rudy.

Don't Spell Like Scooby!

Rokray	**To agree with something that's been said.**
Ruh-roh!	**An exclamation of disbelief and concern.**
Reericious	**Something that tastes good.**
Rexrausted	**To be very, very tired.**
Romerork	**Assignments given by a teacher to be done after school.**
Rencril	**A utensil for writing.**
Rafeteria	**The area where lunch is served.**
Rinciral's Roffice	**A room where naughty children are disciplined.**
Rootrall Rield	**The large grassy yard where sports are played.**

Top Ten Ways to Be a Best Friend

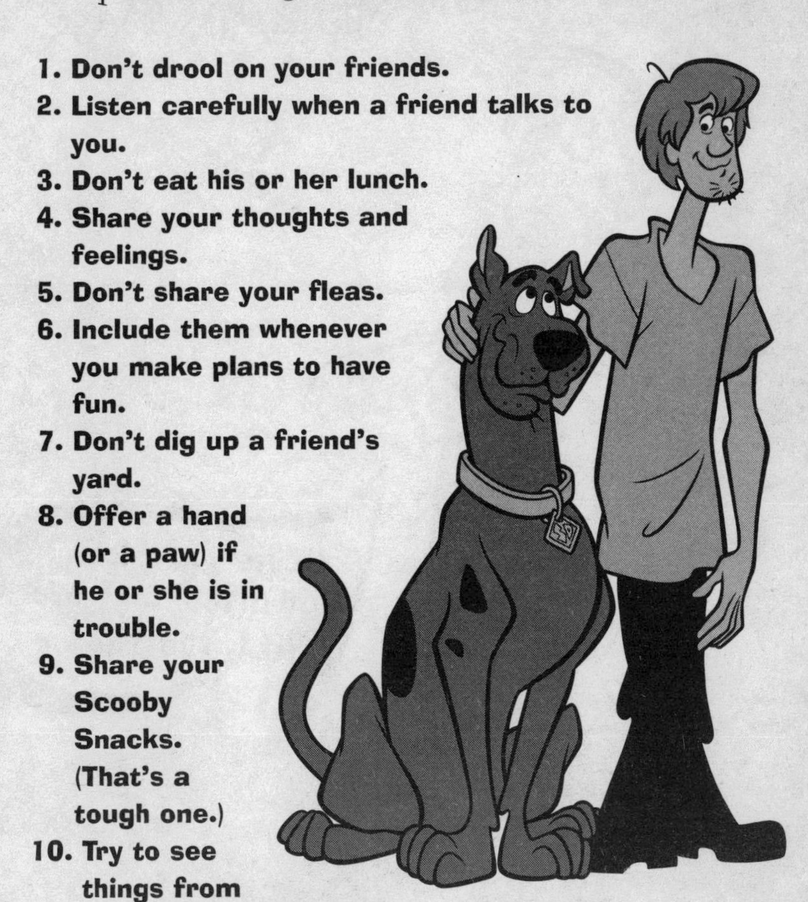

1. Don't drool on your friends.
2. Listen carefully when a friend talks to you.
3. Don't eat his or her lunch.
4. Share your thoughts and feelings.
5. Don't share your fleas.
6. Include them whenever you make plans to have fun.
7. Don't dig up a friend's yard.
8. Offer a hand (or a paw) if he or she is in trouble.
9. Share your Scooby Snacks. (That's a tough one.)
10. Try to see things from your friend's point of view.

Shaggy's Bag

The Mystery Girl

Chapter Four
By Shaggy

Like, whoa. It is just way too soon in the school year to be getting involved in scary chases after mystery girls who never look up and generally seem kinda spooky.

That's about what I was thinking when I jumped into the broom closet to avoid the chase.

"Rr-r-r-aa-h-h-umph!"

"AAAAUUUGHHH," I shouted as I spun around to see who had made that freaky noise.

"Scooby, is that you?"

"Rello."

My trusty dog was hiding in the corner of the closet underneath several brooms.

"Like, sorry for landing on you," I said. "Didn't expect I'd be running into anyone here."

"Rit's roray," Scooby said.

"What are you doing here?"

Before he could answer, the door was flung open.

"YIKES!" I shouted, and Scooby and I bolted out of the closet.

I headed one way and Scooby must have headed the other, because when I turned around, I was all by myself in the hallway.

I thought about looking for the mystery girl, but the idea made me nervous. When I get nervous, I also get hungry. When I get hungry, I really can't do anything until I get something to eat.

So, I headed back to the cafeteria and pulled all my loose change out of my pocket.

I was just about to enjoy a nice milk chocolate candy bar when something brushed up behind me.

"Hey!"

"Zoinks!"

"Calm down, it's just me," Velma said. "What were you doing in that closet with Scooby?"

"Like, what? When? Where?" I didn't want anyone to think I wasn't pulling my weight in the mystery-solving department.

"You've got something on your shirt," Velma said. She picked a long thread off my shoulder.

"Wow," I said, "thread."

"Yes," agreed Velma, "green thread."

She looked at it more carefully. "And it looks like it might have a little corduroy lint attached to it."

"Like, what?" I said.

TO BE CONTINUED

What's Your Nickname?

If your real name was Norville (like mine), you'd probably want a cool nickname, too. My friends started calling me Shaggy because of my haircut.

But there are lots of ways to come up with a new name. I'll give you a few suggestions and you can figure out some far-out names for you and your friends . . . but, like, don't be mean about it.

The most important rule in picking a nickname is this:

BE SURE THE PERSON YOU'RE TALKING ABOUT LIKES THE NAME!!

INITIALS

Sometimes this works, and sometimes it doesn't. Usually first names that start with "J" sound pretty good. For example, if your name is Jack Reilly, you'd be J.R. Sounds cool, right? But if you're me and your name is Norville Rogers, then your initial nickname would be N.R. No way, man. There's just no ring to it.

PART OF A NAME

This could be just the last name or just part of the first or last name. If I hadn't been dubbed Shaggy, I could have been Rog . . . not bad.

BEST FEATURE

This is a cool way to pick a nickname because it's fun and it also might make the person feel good. Think about what a person does well and figure out a name that goes with that. For example, if someone is a straight-A student, he or she could be "Ace." Or if they're really good at math, you could try out "Digit." A good runner could be "Cheetah" or "Flash." A good poet could be "Rhymer." Think about it.

OR JUST ASK . . .

If you and your friends agree that you want nicknames, you could decide that you'll each come up with your own. Then you'll be sure to get exactly the name that describes you best, and you'll also be sure you like it!

Lunchtime Anytime... a Few Thoughts About Food

Let's Hear It for the People Who Pack Our Lunches

I've never known
anything so far-out and fine,
As the moment 'tween
classes when I get to dine.
Give me tuna or chicken
or peanut butter and jelly,
Just make sure there's
plenty to fill up my belly.
As for the other things stuffed
in my sack,
Apples or cookies or anything
you pack,
Don't worry you've pulled too much
off the rack,
What I don't chow for lunch, I'll
keep for a snack.

Swapping Grid — Making an Even Trade?

1 Peanut Butter and Jelly	=1 Ham and Cheese + 1 Cookie
1 Bag of Potato Chips	=1 Bag of Fritos
1 Fruit Wrap	=2 Cookies
1 Roll from school lunch	=Any Sandwich + Milk Money
1 Banana	=1 Apple + 1 Cookie
Crackers and Cheese	=Fruit Cocktail or Half a Sandwich
Carrots	=Nothing!

Of course, you can make your own deals, but, like, make sure you're getting the most out of your lunch, man!

Manners Are Important
OR
Five Things That Are Too Gross Even for Me to Do!

DON'T:

- Lick the bottom of your friend's pudding container.
- Eat your lunch off the floor.
- Stand by the garbage and grab what's being pitched.
- Eat the crumbs off your friend's shirt.
- Save Jell-O for later by putting it in your pocket.

From Shaggy's Kitchen . . .

Once you get through a whole day at school, you deserve a reward! Try this:

Shaggy's Surefire Shake

First thing — fire up the blender (make sure you get permission first).

What you'll need:

Ice cream (you pick the flavor)
Sauce (your choice . . . chocolate, strawberry, butterscotch, whatever!)
Milk
Secret ingredients:
(These are my discoveries — see what you think!)
1 teaspoon vanilla (extract, not ice cream)
1 tablespoon maple syrup

Put into your blender:
2 scoops ice cream
1/4 cup sauce
2 cups milk
Secret ingredients

PUT THE BLENDER LID ON TIGHT! Blend on a medium speed for about 30 seconds. Turn off the blender. Wait for it to stop completely. Check the thickness of the mixture with a spoon to be sure it's just the way you like it. If it's too thin, add a little more ice cream. If it's too thick, blend it a little more.

If you get the okay from your folks, try this groovy after-school snack that'll also be cool in your lunch tomorrow.

Shag-a-licious Sugar Cookies

(Makes about 3 dozen)

Heat oven to 400°F.

Grease a cookie sheet with butter.

In a big bowl, mix these together until they're creamy:

1/2 cup shortening

1 cup sugar

Next, add this stuff into the bowl and mix:

1 egg

2 tablespoons milk

In another bowl, mix these things together:

2 cups flour

1 teaspoon baking powder

1/2 teaspoon salt

1/2 teaspoon baking soda

Now, mix the dry stuff (flour, powder, salt, and soda) in with the shortening mix. Your dough is done!

Use a regular spoon to scoop out balls of dough onto the cookie sheet about two inches apart from each other.

Next, put some sugar on a plate. Grease the bottom of a drinking cup with butter. Then dip the greased glass into the sugar and use it to flatten the dough into round cookies. Bake for eight to ten minutes. Dig in!

Top Ten Ways to Stay Calm Under Pressure

1. Think about breakfast.
2. Think about lunch.
3. Think about dinner.
4. If thinking about meals doesn't help, try thinking about snacks.
5. If thinking about snacks doesn't work, try milk shakes and other liquid nutrients.
6. If all of the above fail to keep you calm, attempt to pass out.
7. Or run as fast as you can away from that thing that's making you nervous.
8. Or get your dog to handle the situation.
9. Or close your eyes, plug your ears, and sing "Jingle Bells."
10. If all of the above fails, you might have to do the one thing I REALLY wouldn't recommend — take a deep breath, face the thing that scares you, and confront and conquer it. Not groovy.

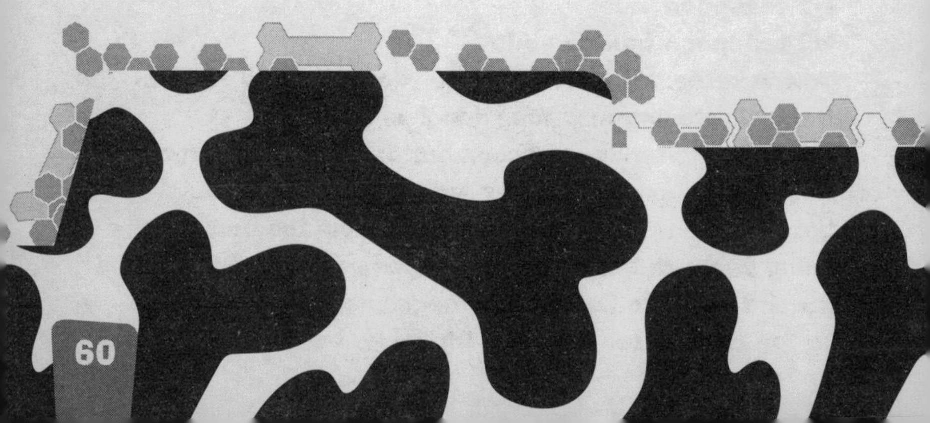

Velma's Advice

The Mystery Girl

Chapter Five
By Velma

The first day of school was history.

I was sitting on a bench in front of school, waiting for the rest of the gang, when I saw Scooby.

"Hey, Scooby," I called. "Nice of you to come pick us up from school."

I could tell he was a little nervous, so I slipped him a Scooby Snack.

"You want to come to school, don't you?" I whispered to him.

He looked at me a little shyly.

"Don't worry. Your secret is safe with me."

I patted him on the head and picked a piece of green lint off his fur.

"You should be careful about this kind of clue," I told him with a smile.

Then I pulled a scarf out of my pocket.

"Aaarrroooff," Scooby gulped.

"You left it in the broom closet," I told him.

Scooby hung his head.

"Dogs aren't allowed in school, Scooby."

"Ri row," he said sadly.

"But I'll tell you what — we'll work together and I'll teach you everything I can. And we'll try to get you a part in the school play, and maybe you can be the football team mascot."

"Rascot! Reah!" Scooby exclaimed.

"I understand wanting to learn and get involved. I think it's great, Scooby, but you really shouldn't be sneaking around the hallways in a costume."

Scooby handed me his paw just as Daphne, Fred, and Shaggy arrived.

"Hey!" Daphne cried. "That's the mystery girl's scarf!"

"Where did you get that?" Fred asked.

"I found it in a broom closet," I said simply. "But there was no sign of the girl."

"Wow," Shaggy said, "it's like she vanished."

"I think that's right," I said. "I don't think we're going to see the mystery girl around anymore."

"What makes you say that?" Daphne asked.

"I don't know," I told her. "I just feel doggone sure. Anyone up for a snack?"

"Like, always!" Shaggy exclaimed.

"Sure," Fred said.

"Sounds good," Daphne agreed.

"Rooooo ret!" Scooby barked.

And we headed to the malt shop.

Velma's Voluminous Vocabulary

A whole bunch of people say I know a whole lot of words. They say I really like to use them, and sometimes it almost sounds like I'm trying to show off. But that's not really true. I think talking with bigger words makes it easier to say a lot of stuff faster than using lots of smaller words. As a teenage braniac crime-fighter, I'm really, really busy and don't have extra time to spend speaking more words than I need to if I can say the same thing with fewer words and still say what I'm trying to say.

Also, I have read some really big books about being extra smart. Those books say that the more words you learn, the more your brain grows and the better it works.

There are other reasons to use as many really big words as you can. It makes you sound smarter and I think people listen to you better when they think you're smart and you know what you're talking about.

So, if you want my advice — I say it's worth studying your new word lists. And don't forget to use the new words whenever you can!

Now, I can say that exact same thing with big words. See how much shorter it is? (And it sounds smarter, too!)

Entire populations have proclaimed my vocabulary enormous. Additionally, they brand my verbiage pretentious. Canard!

I think a large vocabulary allows for more concise communication. As a teenage braniac crime-fighter, I'm overextended and mustn't engage in excessive verbosity to articulate my thoughts.

I've also read volumes on intelligence. They suggest increased language enhances brain growth and function.

There are other reasons to employ a voluminous vocabulary. Others view you as an informed, intelligent individual. Therefore, you're taken more seriously.

So, if you desire my counsel — I recommend an extensive examination of your vocabulary both in study and usage.

Are You a Class-A Detective? Solve This Mini-mystery!

Velma Dinkley headed home from school. She had to hurry if she was going to get a snack in before play practice. She thought about the other things she had to do and was happy that she'd already finished her science homework. She smiled as she patted the left side pocket of her jacket, where it rested safe and sound. But she felt something else in her pocket, too. *Oh, right!* she thought. *I left a Scooby Snack in this pocket last night. Guess I'll have to give it to him when I see him.*

Velma hurried to the malt shop. She hung up her coat on the rack and took a seat at the counter. She had the strangest feeling she was being watched. She put her book bag on the counter in front of her and turned around to look. There was no one there.

"What'll it be?" asked the counterman. "The usual?"

"Yup." She smiled. "French fries with lots of mayonnaise."

As she waited for her fries, she couldn't shake the feeling she was being watched. She looked around again. Jimmy Manning was slumped in the corner booth, staring at her.

"Why is he staring at me?" she wondered. Jimmy had tried to copy her paper during the science exam on Tuesday.

As Velma's French fries arrived, Jimmy approached her. "Want to come over to my house and do our science homework together, Velma?" he asked.

"No thanks, Jimmy. I have other plans this afternoon. Besides, I already . . ." Velma stopped mid-sentence. "I mean . . . Well, I just can't. I have other plans."

"Oh, yeah?" said Jimmy. "Well, thanks for being a pal, Velma! I'll know who to thank when I flunk this class." He charged toward the door. "I should have figured. But we'll see who has the last laugh!" And he was gone.

Jinkies, thought Velma, *get a grip!* Then she looked down at the muddy footprints Jimmy had left on the floor. *And clean your shoes!*

Velma paid for her fries and hurried home to get her play script. The house was empty, so she just ran to her room and grabbed the script.

As she returned to the kitchen, the back door slammed. "Mom?" Velma stopped short. Muddy footprints ran to and from the kitchen table and the door.

That's odd, she thought, glancing at her own clean shoes. She put her script in her bag and hurried out the door.

Daphne and Fred were already at Shaggy's place when Velma got there. They were seated at a large table, ready to start rehearsal. Scooby sat on an old sofa, and watched as Velma took off her gray jacket and laid it next to him. She removed her script from her bag and placed the bag on the bookshelf by the door.

Fred said, "Let's start with scene five in the second act."

"Fine by me," answered Shaggy. "That's my best scene!"

Shaggy began as Old Man Crackitt, his character. "I warned you kids not to come here! But you wouldn't listen and now . . . NOW we'll see who has the last laugh!!"

Just then, the room was plunged into darkness. Everyone started yelling. "HEY!!" "What gives?" "Who doused the lights??!!" Then there was a crash and a chill came over the room as an icy wind blew through the open door.

Shaggy felt for his flashlight. He turned it on and scanned the room. Everyone was still there. But the door was open and all the books from the bookcase were spilled across the floor. Velma's bag was open and the left pocket of her jacket was torn and empty. There was a strange wet substance on the pocket.

Fred checked the electrical box. The power switch had been turned off. A trail of muddy footprints led from the light box to the door. As Fred returned, Velma exclaimed, "My science textbook is missing, and someone has taken my science homework!"

Do you know who took Velma's homework?

Velma told the others about her strange encounter with Jimmy Manning at the malt shop. It was odd that he had said "We'll see who has the last laugh" just as Old Man Crackitt had when the lights went out. She also told them about all the muddy footprints.

"There are muddy footprints here, too!" Fred said, examining the floor.

"That clinches it!" said Daphne. "Jimmy Manning must have taken your homework. He had the motive, and the circumstantial evidence is overwhelming."

They all looked at Velma, who started to grin. "Not so fast," she said. "You're right about several things, but Jimmy Manning could not have been the culprit."

Everyone looked puzzled. It had to be Jimmy, didn't it?

"Jimmy did have the motive," she continued. "He has already shown that he will do anything to keep from failing science class, including cheating on tests. Most likely it was Jimmy who left the footprints in my house. I think I startled him before he could take my book bag, so he left my house and then followed me here."

"But he asked you to help him," said Daphne. "He threatened you. He followed you all over town. Yet he didn't take your homework?"

"No, he didn't," said Velma matter-of-factly. "He couldn't have. And he didn't take my science book, either. I left it at school because I finished my science homework before I left. Jimmy didn't know that I had already done the assignment and put it in my jacket pocket. Naturally, he would have assumed that if I had done it at all, it would be in my book bag. That's why he followed me here and shut off the lights. He rummaged through my bag in the dark, found nothing but my gym clothes, and left."

"So who took it?" everyone cried.

Velma slowly turned to smile at Scooby, who was now sitting on the sofa wearing a very guilty expression.

"**SCOOBY!?**" they all yelled.

"Scooby," said Velma. "It's quite simple, really. I left a Scooby Snack in the same pocket as my homework. When the lights went out, Scooby naturally took advantage of the situation and grabbed for my coat pocket.

Unfortunately, he got more than he bargained for and swallowed my homework as well. I should have given him the snack as soon as I walked in the door."

Scooby coughed and bits of white paper floated from his mouth. "Rorry, Relma."

"And with that," said Velma, laughing, "I think we've got our mystery solved."

Velma's Top Ten Study Tips

1. Take careful notes in class. They'll be your best friend when it comes time to prepare for a test.
2. Have a separate notebook or at least a separate section of your notebook where you write down all assignments.
3. Don't put off studying on weeknights. Try to do it before dinner.
4. On the weekend, try not to wait until Sunday night to get to your homework.
5. Leave yourself enough time for a break while you're studying. It's good to get up and stretch every once in a while.

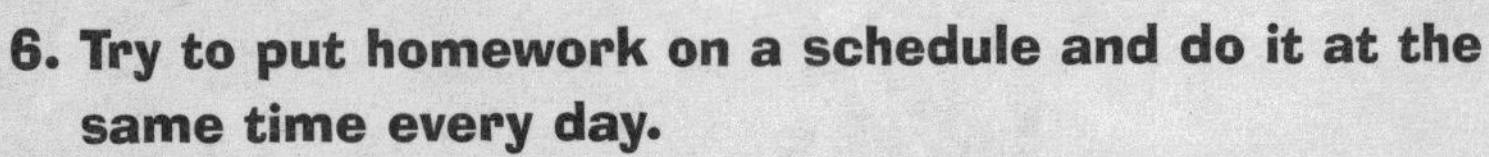

6. Try to put homework on a schedule and do it at the same time every day.
7. Find a study partner who can help quiz you and use flash cards with you.
8. If your study partner is also a good friend, be sure you set aside this time for studying only, not fun and games.
9. The best way to test yourself on something is to try to teach it to someone else. After you think you've studied something long enough, try to explain it to someone else.
10. Take care of yourself — get enough rest, eat healthy food, exercise.

It's all part of being a brainiac!

Take a Look at Yourself . . . What Do You Want to Be?

School is the best place in the world to figure out what you want to do — today and in the future. There are so many ways to have fun and learn a little bit about yourself at the same time.

Do you know what you want to do?

Yes? Then sign up with the club or activity that lets you do it.

No? Then consider the places you could go if you joined . . .

ACTIVITY	CAREER
School Newspaper	Writer, Editor, Photographer
Mentor Program	Teacher
Student Government	Politician, Business-person
Drama Club	Actor, Director, Playwright
Yearbook Committee	Publisher, Advertiser
Band and Choir	Musician, Composer, Teacher
Pep Club	Marketing Person, Artist
Sports	Athlete, Coach

Where do you want to go?

Find the thing you like best and dive in!

Back-to-School Checklist

Do you know who your new teacher is?

Do you have a locker? Locker partner? Do you know who it is?

Have you figured out what you're going to wear?

Do you have enough notebooks and pencils and pens?

Have you thought about what activities and clubs you might get involved with?

Can you name five books you want to read this year?

Do you have any big goals for this year?

You may not know the answers to all of these questions yet, or maybe you do. Either way, a new school year is full of surprises. It's like one big mystery that's up to you to solve!